BLOODLINES

DEPTH CHARGE

written by
M. Zachary Sherman

illustrated by
Raymund Bermudez

colored by
Raymund Lee

STONE ARCH BOOKS
a capstone imprint

DEDICATED TO THE MEN AND WOMEN
OF THE ARMED SERVICES

Bloodlines is published by Stone Arch Books,
A Capstone Imprint, 1710 Roe Crest Drive
North Mankato, MN 56003
www.capstonepub.com

Cataloging-in-Publication Data is available on
the Library of Congress website.
ISBN: 978-1-4342-3764-4 (library binding)
ISBN: 978-1-4342-3876-4 (paperback)
ISBN: 978-1-4342-4196-2 (paperback)

Summary: During World War II, British
Intelligence discovers a German U-505
submarine anchored off the coast of
Denmark. Stashed onboard are invaluable
codebooks, keys to deciphering the enemy's
communications. To secure the documents, a
British commando and U.S. Army Lieutenant
Aaron Donovan must team up, sneak aboard
the enemy submarine, and get off alive!

Art Director: Bob Lentz
Graphic Designer: Brann Garvey
Production Specialist: Michelle Biedscheid

Photo credits: Alamy: INTERFOTO, 63, World
History Archive, 7; AP Images: U.S. Signal
Corps Handout, 21; Getty Images Inc.: Hulton
Archive/FPG, 32, Popperfoto, 72, U.S. Air Force
photo, 20, SSGT Marie Cassetty, 73; M. Zachary
Sherman, 82, back cover; U.S. Army photo by
Himes, 62

Printed in the United States of America
in Stevens Point, Wisconsin.
102011 006404WZS12

TABLE OF CONTENTS

PERSONNEL FILE

FIRST LIEUTENANT
Aaron Donovan

ORGANIZATION:
U.S. Army, Office of Strategic Services

ENTERED SERVICE AT:
Stephens County, Georgia

BORN:
August 28, 1921

EQUIPMENT

Watch Cap

Field Jacket

M1936 Pistol Belt

Ammunition

Sten Mk2 Machine Gun

.45 Caliber Pistol

M1942 First Aid Pouch

Combat Service Boots

OVERVIEW: WORLD WAR II

In 1939, Adolf Hitler and his German army invaded the country of Poland. This ruthless dictator viewed Germans as the "master race." He hoped to exterminate all Jews from Europe and to eventually rule the world. Some countries, including Italy and Japan, joined his evil efforts. They were known as the Axis powers. Others chose to fight against him and his Nazi regime. Those countries, which included Great Britain, the Soviet Union, and the United States, were known as the Allies. To stop German expansion and the genocide of European Jews, the Allied troops could not fail.

ADOLF HITLER

MAP

Norway

Sweden

North Sea

Scotland

Gilleje

Denmark

England

Netherlands

Germany

MISSION

Sneak aboard the German U-505 submarine anchored off the coast of Denmark, steal the Nazi's secret codebooks, and escape alive.

CHAPTER 001

SECRET MISSION

"Are you sure about this, Lieutenant?" General Magruder asked. He clutched a secret radio transcript in his hands.

"Yes, sir," answered First Lieutenant Aaron Donovan. "It's been rechecked and verified, sir." He squinted as he stood in front of his commanding officer. Bright orange sunlight streamed through the drapes behind the general. The sun was setting in Istanbul. The squint couldn't be helped, but it gave the young lieutenant an expression of steely determination. It was expression that the general noted with approval.

As director of the Office of Strategic Services in Istanbul, Turkey, General Richard Magruder oversaw a delicate mission. He commanded U.S. troops that served as spies only a stone's throw from the enemy's backyard, Nazi Germany.

"Tell me the story," ordered the general. He moved from the window and sat behind his huge oak desk.

Donovan handed him a folder containing several photos of a German submarine. "She's sub U-505, sir," he said. "British destroyers stalked her for fifteen hours in the North Sea before she disappeared. It looks like her main engine gave out."

Donovan pointed at the top photo. "From the dark cloud around her aft section," he continued, "we assume she's leaking fuel and is disabled. This presents us with an amazing opportunity, sir."

"An intelligence opportunity?" asked the general, glancing up.

"Exactly, sir," answered Donovan. "As you know, the Germans have added more decoding wheels to their Enigma cipher machine, destroying our ability to decode their messages. But the latest codebooks for every variation of the machine are onboard that sub. If we can get our hands on those codebooks, we'd be able to listen in on the Germans from here to Christmas."

The general grinned. "Where is the sub now?"

"Docked in Gilleleje," replied Donovan. "It's a small fishing village on the east coast of Denmark. WAVE picked up a radio broadcast from the U-boat skipper asking for a special engineering team be sent from Germany to help with repairs."

"I assume you have a plan," the general said.

"We're calling it Operation Deep Six," Donovan answered confidently. "With British help, we'll insert a two-man commando team to intercept those engineers and replace them. Most of the sub's forty-five-man crew will be ashore, with minimal security left on board. While pretending to repair the ship, our men will plant explosives on her ballast tanks, simulate an engine rupture, and scuttle the boat. Then, when the rest of the crew evacuate, our men grab the codebooks and escape."

"And the Brits? Why are we cutting them in on this?"

"They've got contacts in the Danish Resistance that we'll need to successfully get out of Denmark. They've also got an experienced agent who knows these U-boats inside and out. A British commando named Nigel Brett. But it'll still go according to our plan, sir," Donovan said.

"Good work, Lieutenant." The general looked up at the young man and smiled. "When do you leave?"

Donovan's eyes went wide.

* * *

"Why me?" Donovan mumbled, sitting inside a C-47 Skytrain military transport.

"Because you opened your mouth, sir," said Sergeant Hawkesworth of the British Royal Air Force. "That's how the military works — Yank, Brit, or otherwise!"

"What do you mean?" Donovan asked.

"When it's your plan, you end up doing the volunteering without even knowin' it, sir!" said Hawkesworth.

Donovan grinned at the jumpmaster and shifted his seat on the bench. Hawkesworth walked away as another Brit squeezed past him. The new man stood six feet tall, one hundred eighty pounds, and was packed with the same combat gear loading down Donovan. But on him, the American decided, it looked natural. The Brit was Captain Nigel Brett, British Commando and MI6 agent.

His blond hair was cut close to the scalp. He carried his helmet at his side. At first glance, any Allied soldier would have mistaken Brett for a Nazi.

Luckily, that was the plan.

Having been in the war for the past three years, since the British troops began fighting in earnest, Brett had seen a lot of combat. Name a strategic battle and Brett had been neck-deep in it. And always fighting behind enemy lines.

Donovan's entry to the war had been completely different.

After the attack on Pearl Harbor, the three Donovan brothers went to the nearest Army recruiting station to sign up. But when recruiters found out Aaron could speak fluent German, they figured the incredible education in the young man's head would be better suited for the new Intelligence Section, rather than getting spilled out on some French farm somewhere.

Mike ended up in the 101st.

Everett, who always wanted a bigger challenge, hitched up with the Marine Corps.

But for Aaron, the U.S. Army was a perfect fit.

Intelligence work in the Office of Strategic Services, he soon discovered, demanded more of him than just book smarts. Training involved advanced small arms, explosives, knife fighting, boxing — the works. He was learning to be a spy. Then Lieutenant Donovan was made a Lead Analyst, shipped to the Counter Intelligence center in Istanbul, Turkey, and much to his displeasure, placed behind a desk.

For two years he did his part, from advanced code breaking to signals intelligence. Donovan wanted to see more action, but he accepted each task and did the best job he could. And because of this, his peers respected him and his superiors trusted him. Now, however, the desk was gone. The war had grown closer.

The vibrations from the C-47 Skytrain's props shuddered through Donovan's entire body. *Be careful what you ask for,* he told himself.

Captain Brett sat down next to Donovan and smiled. "Glad to see all you Yanks aren't as gung-ho as General Patton back in '42!" Brett said.

"No, but we do our duty all the same," Donovan replied.

"Good," said Brett. He nodded and stared down at his gloves.

Anxiously, Donovan felt his parachute straps, making sure they were locked in place. Once a jumper secures his gear, he knew, he never went over it again. That was for nervous, untrained soldiers. Rechecking was a total rookie mistake.

Brett was watching him.

"How many jumps will this be for you, Lieutenant?" the British captain asked.

"Seventeen," Donovan said.

Brett leaned in closer. "How many combat jumps?" he growled.

Donovan answered quietly. "None."

"For the love of —! Listen very carefully," said Brett. "I was doing this long before Uncle Sam decided to join the party, so if you get me killed, I'm going to haunt you forever. You understand me?"

On the battlefield eight hundred feet below, First Lieutenant Donovan would have operational control over this mission. Superior officer or not, Brett reported to him — not the other way around.

"I may not have the same experience you do —" Donovan started.

"You've got that right," Brett interrupted.

"Which is exactly the point," Donovan continued. "I want men around me who have more experience. Who wouldn't? I specifically requested you for this operation because of your expertise. But I have trained for this, and I was put in charge. So if you're not ready to follow this operation to the letter, you can sit in this tin can while I go down there and secure the codebooks myself. Do you understand me, Captain?"

Brett raised an eyebrow and grinned. "Aye . . . sir."

Brett admired Donovan's spunk, but guts could only get you so far. To think they had assigned him a rookie. It boggled the mind.

"You do at least speak German?" Brett asked snidely.

"*Ja, ich tun,*" answered Donovan.

"Fine. It's your plan, and you're in command. But remember —" Brett pointed to the barrel of the Sten Mk2(S) machine pistol strapped to Donovan's gear. "This end gets pointed at the Nazis."

"Thanks," said First Lieutenant Donovan. "I'll try to remember that."

"Thirty seconds!" the jumpmaster yelled from the cockpit. The two officers glared at one another.

"After you, sir." Brett waved toward the hatch.

Sneering, Donovan stood, clipped his snap hook onto the static line, and moved toward the open door.

The midnight wind whipped through his hair as Donovan stepped into the doorway. He jammed on his helmet and waited for the go signal.

The light turned from red to green.

"Jump!"

He swallowed hard, stepped into the roaring darkness, and let gravity take control.

DEBRIEFING

C-47 SKYTRAIN MILITARY TRANSPORT

SPECIFICATIONS

FIRST FLIGHT: 12-23-1941
WING SPAN: 95 feet 6 inches
LENGTH: 63 feet 9 inches
HEIGHT: 17 feet
WEIGHT: 31,000 lbs.
CRUISE SPEED: 160 mph
MAX RANGE: 3,600 miles
ACCOMMODATION: 3 crew and
6,000 pounds of cargo, or 28
airborne troops, or 14 stretcher
patients with 3 attendants.

HISTORY

In 1941, the Douglas Aircraft
Company modified a version of
their DC-3 airliner for military
use. The C-47 Skytrain became an
essential carrier aircraft during
World War II. By the end of the
war, more than 10,000 had been
built. Some carried equipment,
including fully assembled Jeeps,
37-mm cannons, and medical
supplies. Others carried soldiers
with full combat gear into battle
or returned with wounded vets.
One version of the aircraft, known
as the C-53 Skytroop, dropped U.S.
paratroopers behind enemy lines.

FACT

During World War II, the Douglas
C-47 Skytrain became known by
soldiers as the "Gooney Bird."

PARATROOPERS

DROP ZONE

On August 13, 1940, at Lawson Field in Georgia, Lieutenant William T. Ryder made the first ever U.S. paratroop jump. By 1944, more than 13,000 paratroopers had taken to the skies during World War II. These men were part of Operation Overlord, an extensive military campaign aimed at stopping Nazi Germany. Although they planned to drop behind enemy lines, many were killed in the air or scattered across the dangerous countryside. More than 1,000 paratroopers died during the campaign, and twice as many were injured.

STEN MK2(S)

British 9-mm submachine guns used by British forces throughout World War II. They have a simple design and low production costs. Over 4 million Stens in various versions were made in the 1940s.

CHAPTER 002

INTERCEPT

The night was crisp. Rain clouds loomed overhead. A cool breeze blew in from the ocean to the northwest.

But Donovan didn't feel it. Sweat poured down his forehead as the two Allied commandos silently slinked north toward the small village of Gilleleje. The sweat dripped down the black greasepaint he and Brett had applied to their faces as soon as they landed. Black knit caps curled atop their crew cuts. Dark as shadows, the men each carried a black rucksack, a compact leather utility belt, and a submachine gun.

They blended perfectly into the moonless night.

Making as little noise as possible, Donovan followed the footsteps of his partner as Brett cautiously took point. At every sixth step across the damp ground, Donovan looked behind them. He stared at the dense foliage and rustling pine trees. No one was following.

Denmark, he thought as he glanced around. *Not all that different from Willow Creek, Indiana.*

Except that Indiana wasn't occupied by the German army, or policed by the ruthless Gestapo. Donovan and Brett didn't need to worry about roving patrols of infantry and tanks like the men fighting on the front lines of other European battlefields, but there were many Danes who sympathized with the Germans. If the two were seen by anyone, even Danish locals, they ran the risk of being caught. The mission would be a failure.

Brett, Donovan decided, was a pompous jerk, but he was right about one thing. Donovan was green. He wasn't a field operative with years of battle-hardened missions under his belt, and tonight he was nervous. Nervous about the unknown. About the possibility of getting killed. But more importantly, Donovan was worried about not getting the job done.

Donovan felt the weapon in his palms, wondering if he'd actually have to fire it. He shook his head and wiped sweat from his eyes. Then he cleared his mind of doubt and focused again on the immediate task.

The lieutenant took deep breaths and watched Brett's boots as he followed closely through the pitch-black forest. And, just as he had been trained, at every sixth step he stopped and glanced behind him as they advanced toward the port of Gilleleje.

After three hours, a break in the tree line caught Brett's attention. He signaled Donovan to crouch low. They had reached the road to the village.

Donovan knelt and raised his weapon to his shoulder.

Brett placed his back against a tree and pulled a small map from his right cargo pocket. Unfolding it, he glanced around. This part of the road wasn't paved, but it was well marked. Brett was looking for a waypoint, a landmark. He saw a small white road marker. He looked at the luminous dial of his watch. This was the location of their ambush, but they were behind schedule. They needed to set up quickly.

Brett waved his hand in the air like a crazed third-base coach. Donovan read the signals. Brett wanted the young lieutenant to cross the road, make his way to the far side, set up cover just inside the line of trees, and wait.

Donovan sprinted across the road and hunkered down. The sound of an engine rumbled through the silent woods. Moments later, headlights illuminated the darkened dirt road. A German Volkswagen Kübelwagen drove around a bend. As the car headed straight for them, its tailpipe belched thick clouds of black smoke. It approached the ambush point.

The two Allies had gotten there just in time.

Brett locked eyes with Donovan. Brett stared at him sternly and then slid back the bolt of his gun. Across the road, Donovan did the same. Then he saw Brett reach into a pouch on his utility belt.

With the flick of a wrist, several spikes soared from Brett's hand and littered the road. The sound of the metal was muffled in the hard dirt and could not be heard above the engine of the German car.

The Kübelwagen's front left tire suddenly exploded in a small puff of white dust. The vehicle lost control. It skidded off the road and onto the small muddy shoulder, a mere yard from Donovan's position.

The doors opened with a burst of angry German. The driver and his passenger bent over the wheel wells to inspect the damage. The driver suddenly stopped. His boot scraped against something in the dirt. He reached down and picked up a road spike. His eyes went wide.

"Gewehre!" he yelled.

The Germans reached for the black Lugers at their belts. Then Donovan and Brett sprang from cover and fired.

POW! POW! POW

Silenced shots spit from the weapons. Donovan saw the impact and heat from each slug. The Germans' knees buckled, and then both men dropped to the ground.

Then, as suddenly as it had started, the battle was over. Silence reclaimed the forest. Donovan looked across the narrow road at the Brett.

Though he tried to hold back, Donovan's emotions were too powerful to stay bottled up. His bottom lip quivered. His hands shook as he gripped the submachine gun. Then tears streaked from his eyes.

"First time?" Brett asked him quietly.

Donovan nodded slowly. He reached up and wiped the wetness from his cheeks.

"It gets easier," Brett said. He slung his weapon and gripped the armpits of the nearest dead German. Then he dragged the limp figure off the road and into the shadows of the nearby trees.

Donovan looked down at the body of the second Nazi lying on the ground.

"That's what scares me," he said softly.

DEBRIEFING

NAZI GERMANY

HISTORY

The Nazi Party, or National Socialist German Workers' Party, ruled Germany from 1933 to 1945. It was led by Adolf Hitler, a feared dictator who sought to expand Germany's influence around the globe and "cleanse" the world of all "inferior" races. For a time, he succeeded. After invading Poland in 1939, Germany expanded its control across most of Europe and Northern Africa through a series of violent military campaigns. They also killed millions of Jews and other minorities during the genocide known as the Holocaust.

DUTCH RESISTANCE

Despite the Netherlands neutrality in World War II, Nazi Germany invaded the country on May 10th, 1940. French forces and British ships came to the Netherlands' aid, but quickly retreated after helping to evacuate many civilians and several thousand prisoners of war. After the bombing of Rotterdam, the majority of the Dutch army surrendered on May 14th, 1940, although a small force continued to occupy part of Zeeland.

VOLKSWAGEN KÜBELWAGEN

HISTORY

In many ways, the lightweight Kübelwagen was the German equivalent of the American Jeep during World War II. Both served as reliable, cost-efficient vehicles used to transport VIPs short to medium distances – on or off-road. The windowless doors served as exit points for German soldiers in case of an attack or ambush. By the end of World War II, somewhere between 50,000-55,000 Kübelwagens were produced.

FIRST DRIVEN: 1936
ENGINE: 23-25 horsepower air-cooled four-speed depending on make
TOP SPEED: 50 mph
ACCOMMODATION: One driver and three passengers.

FACT

The Volkswagen Kubelwagen's name is short for *Kübelsitzwagen*, which means "bucket seat car" in German.

LUGER P08 PISTOL

HISTORY

Also known as the Pistole Parabellum 1908, the Luger P08 is a semi-automatic pistol that was designed by Georg J. Luger in 1898. The Luger was a preferred firearm amongst Germans in World War I and World War II. It uses the popular 9x19-mm Parabellum cartridge. The weapon was known for its accuracy and unique appearance, and is still popular today among collectors.

FIRST USED: 1900
IN SERVICE: 1908-1945, Germany
WEIGHT: 1.92 lbs.
LENGTH: 8.75 inches
BARREL LENGTH: 3.9-8.02 inches
EFFECTIVE RANGE: 165 feet
FEED SYSTEM: 8-round box magazine

CHAPTER 003

U-505

Winds off the Baltic Sea weren't especially cold that time of year, but First Lieutenant Donovan sat shivering in the front seat of the Kübelwagen.

Having wiped the black greasepaint from their faces, he and Brett were now wearing exact copies of the German engineers' uniforms. Donovan shuffled slowly through the personal effects they'd pulled off the bodies: I.D. papers, travel documents, handwritten letters to loved ones that would never be sent.

Brett could tell it was eating at the young American. "Shake it off, Yank. Had to be done," said the captain. He steered the stolen vehicle through the countryside.

It's not that easy, thought Donovan. He'd killed a man in cold blood. No matter the reasons, that German was dead and it was his fault. "They were just standing there, defenseless. How could we —" the first lieutenant began.

Brett slammed on the brake. "We're soldiers," he shouted. "We've taken an oath to stop Hitler from taking over this planet. If killing a couple of Nazi engineers gets us one step closer to that goal, then I'll do it again with a smile on my face. Now either get on board or get out!"

Brett's blue eyes gleamed like steel in the early morning light. A long moment passed. Brett took a deep breath and let it out slowly.

"We're at war," he said softly. "We do things we're not always proud of." Donovan wasn't looking at him, but the Brit's voice seemed to change. "Lots of things."

Brett stepped on the gas.

"Yeah?" said Donovan quietly.

"Let's just say I'm not getting into heaven any time soon. But my son will. A long time from now, and not at the hands of some dirty SS Stormtrooper." Brett turned onto a paved road. "You asked, 'how could we?'"

Donovan nodded.

"I'll tell you how. I do it for my son. I do it for Ian," said the captain.

Donovan stared out the windshield. Brett's remarks reminded him of what his teacher back at the academy had said: "The needs of the many outweigh the needs of the few."

He and Brett were specks of dust in this war. Each soldier was called on to give everything, and it was all to protect a greater good. The families back home. The townspeople of Gilleleje. The freedom of whole countries, like Denmark. His and Brett's lives earned meaning by their deeds, and by their personal sacrifices.

"I —" Donovan started, but there were no words, and first lieutenant played it off. "I, uh, can't see. It's too dark in here." Donovan held up the documents, trying to read them better.

Reaching into his pocket, Brett produced a brass lighter and handed it to Donovan.

"Impressive," Donovan said as he struck a flame.

"My father gave me that," said Brett. "He kept it until he came back from Germany in 1919. I'll pass it on to my son, but hopefully he never has to use it like we are."

Donovan returned his attention to the pile in his lap. "Personal papers, passes, engineering specs for the sub," he mumbled, flipping through it. "Orders."

He cracked open the envelope and read the commands carefully. Suddenly, he smiled. "Yes, we got the right men," Donovan said.

"Hooray for our side," said Brett, drily.

Donovan fished out a set of papers from his gear. He compared them to the ones found on the Germans.

Perfect, he thought. The studio shots of Brett and Donovan were an exact match in texture, grain, and lighting to the Nazi photographs. He was proud of his men. They had worked long and hard on these forgeries.

"What's our exit strategy?" Brett asked.

"Once we exit the sub, Danish Resistance will meet us on shore in a truck with a Blue Star Vodka logo," said Donovan. "They'll take us cross-country to an airstrip. A small commercial plane will fly us to England."

"Excellent," replied Brett. "Look, we've got about two hours before we hit the village. Try to get some rest."

After folding the papers, Donovan placed them in his shirt and crossed his arms. Within seconds, he was asleep.

*   *   *

The rising sun crested over the waters of Gilleleje, casting a golden glow on the small fishing village. The town's citizens were already awake and moving. Men of all ages prepared fishing nets and carried poles to boats as the trawlers readied to cast off.

All in all, it was a very picturesque morning. Except for the steel behemoth docked not too far away. The gunmetal gray submarine U-505 sat like a wounded whale in the harbor, its hull baking in the hot sun.

On the sub's deck, a twin 20-mm Flack anti-aircraft gun was manned by a single German soldier, watching over the boat for any signs of trouble from air or land. The deck officer was perched atop the conning tower, scanning the shoreline through a pair of field glasses.

On the road next to the dock sat the Kübelwagen. Donovan and Brett geared up as they looked across the water at the sub.

Since the U-505 was 100 yards away from the dock, anchored in deeper waters, they would have to pilot a small rowboat over to the ship and embark from there.

"Just as I thought," Donovan said in German. "We'll have to row out to her. The port's too shallow."

"You ready?" Brett asked in German as he slid the bricks of dynamite into Donovan's satchel.

Nodding, First Lieutenant Donovan adjusted his engineering uniform. "Let's go," he confirmed.

The morning sun was bright and sharp, glinting cheerfully off windows, church steeples, and rain puddles. The two men emerged from their vehicle and walked toward the dock. Brett scanned every detail, mentally creating an escape route in case something went wrong. An empty rowboat lay several yards away.

A German soldier stepped in front of them. "Papers, please, gentlemen," he said in German.

Donovan and Brett reached into their pockets. They presented the soldier with their forged documents.

Slowly, casually, Brett reached into the pockets of his jacket as if he were warming his hands.

In the right pocket nestled a small Walther PPK, fully loaded. The sleek pistol was German-made, but it could do just as much damage in an American hand.

The soldier carefully read through the documents. He looked the men over slowly. Brett and Donovan returned his gaze, expressionless. Finally, the German smiled, and handed back their papers.

"The captain will be happy to see you." He motioned to the small boat. "Climb aboard."

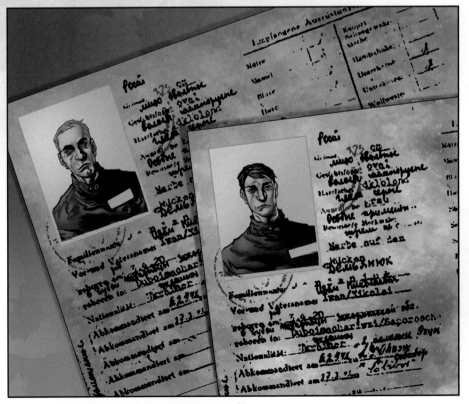

U-505 SUBMARINE

SPECIFICATIONS

MAKE: Type IXC submarine
DISPLACEMENT: 1,120 tons surfaced, 1,232 tons submerged
LENGTH: 252 feet
HEIGHT: 30 feet 10 inches
SPEED: 20.9 mph while surfaced, 8.3 mph submerged
TEST DEPTH: 750 feet
CAPACITY: 48 to 56 people
ARMAMENT: 6 torpedo tubes, 1 105-mm deck gun

FACT

The U-505 was a U-boat built for service by the Germans during World War II.

CAPTURED SUB

U-505 was captured by the United States Navy in June of 1944. Onboard were the Nazi codebooks, the Enigma machine, and other secret materials that greatly assisted code-breaking operations for the Allied forces. All but one of U-505's German crew were captured alive by the Navy task group, and they were interned at a U.S. prisoner of war camp to prevent discovery of the sub's capture by the Germans. U-505 was one of six U-boats that were captured by Allied forces during World War II.

ENIGMA MACHINE

An Enigma machine is one of the cipher machines used to create secret messages by using encryption and decryption, or codes. German engineer Arthur Scherbius invented Enigma toward the end of World War I. It was adopted by Nazi Germany for World War II. It uses a keyboard, a set of rotating discs called rotors, and one of various stepping components to turn one or more of the rotors with each key press.

ULTRA

In December 1932, the Polish Cipher Bureau broke Nazi Enigma cipher codes. Because of this achievement, Allied codebreakers were able to decrypt many secret messages that had been created using the Enigma. The intelligence gleaned from this source was called "Ultra" by the British, and made a substantial contribution to the war effort.

FACT

The Polish Cipher Bureau cracked the Enigma cipher nearly 7 years before the outbreak of World War II.

CHAPTER 004

SABOTAGE

Two hours later, Donovan and Brett were neck-deep in grease, oil, and charred engine parts in the cramped rear of the sub. They were doing what they could to "affect repairs." At least, that's what they hoped all their banging and ripping apart and German cursing looked like to an outsider.

Donovan had a simple knowledge of engines. He had fixed cars in high school. Luckily, Brett knew considerably more. He had attended engineer training with MI6 agents, and knew how to sabotage German equipment as well as repair it.

The U-505's chief engineer peered over his shoulder and scratched his head. "So?" he asked, as Brett threw a very large piece of charred metal behind him.

Brett shook his head. "Not good. She'll need dry-dock to make her seaworthy," he began.

"You'll be lucky to get to France without some English ship sinking you," Donovan finished, faking his disappointment with the machine.

"Batteries could get us to Norway, but not to France, yes?" asked the German.

Donovan nodded.

The German engineer rolled his eyes. "See? That is what I told the captain. But no, he wanted specialists from Berlin to tell him."

"Absolutely," Donovan said. "We hear that all the time."

"We're all just doing Hitler's bidding, eh?" said Captain Brett, jokingly.

But the engineer squinted. It seemed an odd phrase, one a high-ranking German engineer wouldn't say.

"Yes. Where did you say you were from?" the engineer asked suspiciously.

First Lieutenant Donovan looked at his wristwatch. "We've got work to do, and we're running out of time," he snapped. "Now either help us, or get out of the way."

Startled at Donovan's tone, the chief engineer stumbled slightly as he took a step back and saluted. "Yes, sir. I'm sorry, I didn't mean to insult you."

And with that, he was gone.

Grinning, Brett turned from the engine. "Nice one," he whispered.

"Thanks. Here." Donovan handed him the satchel with the dynamite. "Set timers for 1800 hours. That's when the radio guys swap duties."

Impressed, Captain Brett looked at him. "How do you know that?" he asked.

Donovan shrugged. "I read the duty roster in the control room as we came down the ladder."

"Nicely done," Brett whispered. Then he leaned forward and carefully placed the first charge deep within the framework of the engine.

Donovan checked his watch again. They had fifteen minutes before the first charge would go. During that time, he needed to attach a second charge to the ballast tanks in the forward section.

A two-fisted punch would ensure that the ship sank.

"Go on ahead," Brett said. "I'll meet you near the radio room in ten minutes."

Donovan backed out of the narrow engine room. He passed through the enlisted galley where three men sat, including the chief engineer. Nodding quickly he kept going. His boots soon thudded against cross-sectioned steel deck plates. He was over the main ballast tanks.

Donovan knelt and pretended to tie his bootlaces. Without moving his head, he eyeballed his surroundings, confirmed that only the three men were nearby, and then slowly reached into his jacket. He pulled out a specially prepared block of dynamite. It had been shaped to slip in between the deck plates and magnetically stick to the tanks.

"Did you fall, sir?" a voice asked from behind him. The chief engineer came up to Donovan.

Caught off guard, Donovan fumbled. The dynamite block slipped from his grasp and landed on the tank below him with a loud clank.

But he hadn't had a chance to set the detonator.

Springing up, Donovan turned and growled. "No, Sergeant!" he shouted. "Bootlaces do come undone. It is a matter of maintaining order, yes? Not unlike the conditions of your engine room. I have seen children's bedrooms that are cleaner. Don't think that Berlin will not hear about that in my report!"

"Yes, sir!" The engineer was flustered. "May I get you some coffee, sir? Our ship stores are from Brazil."

"Coffee?" Donovan repeated. He bent his head, as if thinking. He was glancing at his watch. Only five minutes before the engineering explosion erupted.

Captain Brett emerged from the room at the other end and entered the galley just as the engineer was scrambling for a cup and saucer. Eyes wide, he glanced at Donovan and then at the engineer.

Donovan shrugged slightly.

Finally, Brett stepped up, placed a hand on the big German's shoulder, and whispered in his ear. "The lieutenant seems a bit high-strung already," he said.

"I don't think he needs the caffeine, do you?" he added with grin. Then Brett pulled a pack of cigarettes from his jacket.

"Would you like to join me for a smoke instead, lieutenant? A bit of fresh air always does good, eh?" He stared at Donovan.

"Certainly, Sergeant."

"Dunhill?" the engineer said as he caught a glimpse of Brett's cigarettes. "Where did you get those?"

Brett smiled. "Off the body of an Englander I killed in South Africa," he said.

"And what was a submarine engineer doing in South Africa?" asked the German.

The other men at the table rose. One of them rested a hand on his sidearm. They inched closer to the main hatchway between engineering and the command section. Donovan saw a ship's clock. Mere seconds now.

Brett lifted his chin and stepped back through the hatch. "What was I doing?" he said in English. "Killing Nazis."

None of the crew had a chance to respond as a massive explosion ripped through the engine room. A fireball barreled down the galley, engulfing the Nazis in a wall of flame.

Brett grabbed Donovan and yanked him through the hatch. He secured the metal door just as the fire was about to reach them. Donovan reached over and slapped the ALARM button on the wall. Red lights flashed in the darkness as Donovan and Brett scurried to the radio room.

Captain Lieutenant Peter Zschech was on the conning tower when the blast occurred. Smoke, men, and waves of heat rushed out the main hatches, vacating the ship. "What's happening?" he demanded as his first officer ran up to him.

"There was an explosion in engineering!" answered the first officer.

"Sound the evacuation!" ordered Captain Zschech. "Get all the men off the ship!"

Below them, the two commandos stormed into the radio room.

An operator was placing the codebooks into a locker when he looked up and saw the two men. "What do you want?" he asked.

Brett knocked the German onto the deck with a strong right hook. Donovan grabbed the codebooks and stuffed them in his pack. "Let's go!" the lieutenant said.

They swiftly made their way to the front of the ship. Their plan was working. The entire sub was being evacuated. And luckily, when they reached the torpedo room, it was deserted.

* * *

After climbing the ladder and popping the hatch, Donovan and Brett emerged on the forward deck, near the bow of the submarine.

Several men were topside, trying to board the same rowboat that had carried Brett and Donovan to the sub. Many of the crew were diving into the cold water. Others were already swimming away from the vessel toward their shipmates onshore.

At the docks, about thirty yards away from the Kübelwagen, a small five-ton truck sat unnoticed under a large tree. A big blue star was emblazoned on the side of the cargo tarp.

"There's our ride," Brett said. He nodded over to the nearby truck.

"Swim?" Donovan asked.

Suddenly, the Brit's eyes went wide. Climbing out of the main hatch was the radio operator he had punched. The man, blood streaming from his broken nose, staggered to the top of the ladder and collapsed.

As the captain bent to help him, the operator waved his hands and tried to speak. He pointed toward the two Allies.

The German captain swiveled his head and locked eyes with Brett. "Halt!" he yelled. "Stop!"

Brett strapped the bag to his back and slapped Donovan on the shoulder. "Always loved the water," said the captain. "Let's go!"

The two men plunged into the harbor and swam toward shore.

The captain yelled at his first officer and pointed at the commandos swimming away from the sub.

The first officer slid down the main ladder and hit the main deck. He grabbed the nearest sailor by his shirt collar. Then he shoved him toward the twin 20-mm Flack gun. *"Erschiessen!"* he ordered. "Shoot!"

Donovan and Brett clambered onto shore. Donovan fell onto the grass, his wet uniform weighing him down.

POW!

POW!

POW!

Flak bullets chipped up all around them.

"Go, go, go!" Captain Brett screamed. He pulled a Walther from his bag.

Several yards ahead of them, the truck driver heard the shouts and the gunfire. He quickly cranked the engine. Thick, gray smoke boiled from its tailpipe, and the truck slowly rolled forward.

On the dock, other German soldiers stood and stared in surprise as the two engineering experts from Berlin bolted across the road, chased by anti-aircraft fire.

"Hit them, you fool!" the first officer yelled at the German sailor.

"I'm just a cook, sir!" the sailor explained as he yanked the charging handle and reloaded the weapon. He pulled the trigger. There was a click, then nothing.

"I think it's jammed, sir!" the sailor said.

"Imbecile!" the first officer said. Framing his mouth with his hands, he yelled to the men on the dock. "Stop them! They're spies!"

Donovan and Brett ran for their lives as the skeleton crew of the U-505 began chasing them. The dock's security forces pulled out MP40s and started firing.

RATATATATATATA

DEBRIEFING

CASUALTIES OF WORLD WAR II

HISTORY

With a total of more than 60 million casualties, World War II was the deadliest conflict in history. Many of these deaths were innocent civilians, including six million Jews and other minorities killed during the Holocaust. Some countries, including Lithuania and Poland, lost nearly 15 percent of their total population in the war.

FACT

Historians estimate that nearly 5 million prisoners of war died while still in captivity during WWII.

STATISTICS

Nearly 60 countries suffered losses during WWII. Here are some of the gruesome totals:

COUNTRY	TOTAL DEATHS
China	10–20 million
Dutch East Indies	3–4 million
France	570,000
Germany	6–9 million
Japan	2.7 million
Poland	5.5–6 million
Soviet Union	24 million
United Kingdom	450,000
United States	420,000

MP40 MACHINE GUN

HISTORY

During World War II, Germany developed the MP40, which stood for *Maschinenpistole*, or Machine Pistol. Designed by Heinrich Vollmer, this lightweight submachine gun quickly became a Nazi-killing machine. The fully automatic, open-bolt design enabled the gun to discharge 550 rounds per minute. Even in the 1940s, this rate of fire was fairly slow. However, the decrease in speed allowed for increased accuracy when firing single shots – an advantage in the short-range, urban-combat situations in European cities.

SPECIFICATIONS

FIRST USED: 1939
MANUFACTURER: Erma Werke
TYPE: Submachine gun
LENGTH: 32.8 inches
WEIGHT: 8.82 lbs.
RANGE: 328 feet
NUMBER BUILT: 1 million
RATE OF FIRE: 500 rounds/minute

FINAL MISSION

Brett and Donovan closed in on the moving truck. The back of the vehicle exploded to life. Whipping the flaps aside, four Danish Resistance members leaned out and aimed machine guns over the pair's heads, firing straight at the Nazis.

"Come on, Yankee!" one of the Resistance members yelled as Donovan neared the truck.

German bullets ricocheted off asphalt.

The Resistance member grabbed Donovan and yanked him into the truck.

Donovan turned. Brett was right behind him. He put his hand out as Donovan braced himself on the tailgate.

"Brett, stop screwing around!" Donovan yelled.

Brett turned as he ran. He opened up on the Germans, dropping two of them.

Then Brett spun back toward the truck and ran at full speed. He reached out his hand. He was inches from Donovan's straining fingers. The American was leaning dangerously far out of the truck toward his friend.

POP!

Immense pain stabbed through Brett's body. He stumbled as his left leg gave out on him. Blood flowed from his thigh and spattered darkly on the road. Donovan's hand moved farther and farther away as the truck moved off.

Donovan screamed over the gunfire, "We have to stop! He's been hit!"

BANG! BANG!

An MP40 bullet flew past him and pierced a Resistance member's head. The Dane flopped back inside the truck, knocking into one of his comrades.

"If we stop, we all die!" another Dane yelled. The remaining three fighters poured gunfire at the pursuing Nazis, closing in on Brett.

Brett limped behind them. "Keep going!" he shouted. He pulled the satchel with the codebooks from his back and held it in his hands.

"I won't leave you behind!" Donovan screamed.

"Catch!" said Brett.

The Brit threw the bag and it sailed toward the back of the truck. Stretching as far as he could, Donovan leaned out, hands open.

The bag soared about a foot away from Donovan's fingertips, fell to the road, and tumbled over and over. The stolen codebooks spilled from its open flap.

The throw was short.

Brett's face fell, defeated.

As he slowed his pace, Nazi bullets caught up with him. He pitched onto the road, face first. Blood pooled around his body.

"Ian," he whispered quietly.

And then he was gone.

A Resistance member held back the struggling Donovan as the truck barreled down the road and fled into the countryside.

DEBRIEFING

INVASION OF NORMANDY

HISTORY

On July 6, 1944, more than 160,000 U.S. troops and other Allied soldiers stormed the beaches of Normandy, France. They attempted to overtake German strongholds in the area. After many casualties, including nearly 2,500 U.S. soldiers, they succeeded. That date, now known as D-Day, became a turning point in the war. During the next year, Allied forces continued to regain territory and push the German army back within its borders. On April 30, 1945, realizing he had lost, Adolf Hitler killed himself. A week later, the war in Europe was officially over.

SURRENDER

Even as the war in Europe ended, battles continued to rage in the Pacific Ocean. Japan, who had attacked Pearl Harbor, Hawaii, in December 1941, refused to give up. Even after heavy losses, Japanese soldiers continued to fight. Then, in August 1945, the United States dropped atomic bombs on the Japanese cities of Hiroshima and Nagasaki. More than 100,000 people were killed. Japan surrendered. On September 2, 1945, World War II was officially over.

NORMANDY AMERICAN CEMETERY

HISTORY

The United States suffered heavy losses during WWII. The largest number of deaths came on July 6, 1944, during the invasion of Normandy, now known as D-Day. Today, 9,387 soldiers still rest on European soil at the American Cemetery and Memorial in Colleville-sur-Mer, Normandy, France. The 172-acre cemetery overlooks Omaha Beach, where U.S. troops stormed ashore during their D-Day assault. Of the deaths that day, 1,557 Americans were never located or identified. A memorial wall at the cemetery honors these unknown soldiers.

WWII MEMORIAL

On April 29, 2004, the National World War II Memorial opened in Washington, D.C. This site, located near the Washington Monument, honors the 16 million U.S. soldiers who served during WWII and the more than 400,000 who were killed. The memorial features 56 granite pillars, two 43-foot arches, a large fountain, and a reflecting pool. Operated by the National Park Service, the memorial has averaged more than 4.4 million visitors each year since its dedication.

CHAPTER 005

EPILOGUE

Operation Deep Six was a failure. Though the mission hadn't yielded the results General Magruder and his peers had hoped for, however, it was discovered later that the explosive device set by Brett in the ship's main engine had been a success. The resulting blast had done its damage. When the U-505 returned to duty after months in dry-dock, her capacity for speed and escape maneuvers had dramatically declined.

Brett's sabotage yielded another positive result. The weakened sub was finally captured on June 4th, 1944. Fifty-eight German sailors were taken prisoner, and the Enigma codebooks were finally secured.

Donovan was sent back to Turkey and back to his desk. Although his mission did not succeed, he was commended and promoted to captain for his efforts.

But none of that mattered to Aaron Donovan as he stood on the doorstep of a quiet cottage on the outskirts of London, a small package in his hands.

Nervously, he rapped on the door and waited. He tugged at the small wrinkles on his uniform. After a short time, he heard the sound of a lock unbolting, and the door opened.

Donovan hurriedly removed his cap and opened his mouth to speak, but stopped short. He looked down. In front of him stood a young boy, about seven years old, blond with blue eyes.

Donovan's mouth ran dry. He stood and stared, unable to speak, not sure what to say even if he could.

"Sir?" the boy said, gazing up at the tall American.

Donovan didn't answer. He was surprised at how much the young boy looked like his father.

"Ian, go back upstairs and play now," rang out a woman's voice. Elizabeth Brett came to the door. The boy stayed beside her, interested in the strange man.

"Is it about Nigel?" she asked softly, holding onto the door for support.

"My name is Captain Aaron Donovan, ma'am. I served with your husband."

She nodded. Though she stood strong, her eyes began to water, the breath caught in her throat.

Donovan held out the small package. "These were his. I just thought you should have them."

Elizabeth fumbled with the box. Inside were some of Brett's personal effects, including his brass trench lighter.

Elizabeth did not look up. "Were you with him?" she asked. "At the end?"

"Yes, ma'am, I had that honor," Donovan replied.

She picked up the small metal object. "It was Nigel's father's," she said. "He always wanted it to go to his son. But Ian's not going to be a soldier."

"No, ma'am," Donovan said. "I know he didn't want him to be."

Mrs. Brett blinked and stared at Donovan. "He told you that?"

"Yes, ma'am, he did."

She took a deep breath. "I think he would have wanted you to have this." She held out the lighter.

"I can't, ma'am," said Donovan.

"Please," she said. "You were his friend."

Donovan remembered when Brett had handed him the lighter in the Kübelwagen back in the Danish forest. "Hopefully, my son will never have to use it like we are," Brett had said.

Slowly, Donovan took it from her and placed it in his pocket. "Thank you," he said. "I know how much this meant to him."

"They told me he was killed in the line of duty," she said. "But they didn't tell me more than that —" Tears began sliding down her cheeks. Her hands shook as she clutched the box.

"It was a top-secret mission," said Donovan.

"Regulations don't allow them to reveal anything else. But —" he hesitated. "I think you deserve to know the truth. I think you deserve to know how he died."

Opening the door, the woman held out a hand.

"And I think you deserve to know how he lived," she said.

Taking her hand in his, Captain Aaron Donovan entered the Brett family home and closed the door softly behind him.

EXTRAS

ABOUT THE AUTHOR

M. ZACHARY SHERMAN is a veteran of the United States Marine Corps. He has written comics for Marvel, Radical, Image, and Dark Horse. His recent work includes *America's Army: The Graphic Novel, Earp: Saint for Sinners*, and the second book in the SOCOM: SEAL Team Seven trilogy.

AUTHOR Q&A

Q: Any relation to the Civil War Union General William Tecumseh Sherman?

A: Yes, indeed! I was one of the only members of my family lineage to not have some kind of active duty military participation – until I joined the U.S. Marines at age 28.

Q: Why did you decide to join the U.S. Marine Corps? How did the experience change you?

A: I had been working at the same job for a while when I thought I needed to start giving back. The biggest change for me was the ability to see something greater than myself; I got a real sense of the world going on outside of just my immediate, selfish surroundings. The Marines helped me to grow up a lot. They taught me the focus and discipline that helped get me where I am today.

Q: When did you decide to become a writer?

A: I've been writing all my life, but the first professional gig I ever had was a screenplay for Illya Salkind (*Superman* 1-3) back in 1995. But it was a secondary profession, with small assignments here and there, and it wasn't until around 2005 that I began to get serious.

Q: Has your military experience affected your writing?

A: Absolutely, especially the discipline I have obtained. Time management is key when working on projects, so you must be able to govern yourself. In regards to story, I've met and been with many different people, which enabled me to become a better storyteller through character.

Q: Describe your approach to the Bloodlines series. Did personal experiences in the military influence the stories?

A: Yes and no. I didn't have these types of experiences in the military, but the characters are based on real people I've encountered. And those scenarios are all real, just the characters we follow have been inserted into the time lines. I wanted the stories to fit into real history, real battles, but have characters we may not have heard of be the focus of those stories. I've tried to retell the truth of the battle with a small change in the players.

Q: Any future plans for the Bloodlines series?

A: There are so many battles through history that people don't know about. If they hadn't happened, the world would be a much different place! It's important to hear about these events. If we can learn from history, we can sidestep the mistakes we've made as we move forward.

Q: What's your favorite book? Favorite movie? Favorite video game?

A: My favorite book is *The Maltese Falcon* by Dashiell Hammett; I love a good mystery with hard-boiled detectives! As for movie, hands-down it's *Raiders of the Lost Ark*. It is a fantastic story of humanity winning out over evil and the characters are real people thrown into impossible odds. Lots of fun! As for games, there are way too many to mention, but I love sci-fi shooters and first-person games.

EXTRAS

ABOUT THE ILLUSTRATORS

Raymund Bermudez was born and raised in Quezon City, Philippines. After studying architecture for a couple years, he to took up fine arts at the University of the Philippines, focusing on illustration. Since 1998, he's worked on a variety of projects as a freelance illustrator.

Raymund Lee is a comic book colorist based in Manila, Philippines. He got his first break working on the popular Stone and Aria comics. Eventually, he conquered the pages of Marvel comics, including Wolverine, the Uncanny X-Men, and other top titles. His coloring style varies depending on the artwork. A big movie fan, this veteran colorist treats every page or panel as if taken from a movie scene. When not working, he enjoys spending time with his family and two pugs.

THE PROCESS

A CALL TO ACTION

WORLD WAR II

BLOODLINES
DEPTH CHARGE

M. ZACHARY SHERMAN

During World War II, British Intelligence discovers a German U-505 submarine anchored off the coast of Denmark. Stashed onboard are invaluable codebooks, keys to deciphering the enemy's communications. To secure the documents, a British commando and U.S. Army First Lieutenant Aaron Donovan must team up, sneak aboard the enemy submarine, and get off alive!

KOREAN WAR

BLOODLINES
DAMAGE CONTROL

M. ZACHARY SHERMAN

During the Korean War, a U.S. Army cargo plane crashes behind enemy lines, and soldiers of the 249th Engineer Battalion are stranded. Facing a brutal environment and attacks by enemy forces, Private First Class Tony Donovan takes action! With spare parts and ingenuity, he plans to repair a vehicle from the wreckage and transport his comrades to safety.

VIETNAM WAR

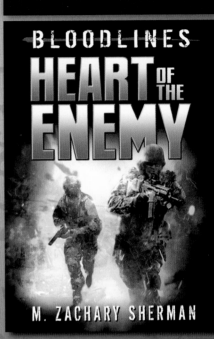

BLOODLINES

EMERGENCY OPS

M. ZACHARY SHERMAN

IRAQ WAR

BLOODLINES

HEART OF THE ENEMY

M. ZACHARY SHERMAN

During the Vietnam War, Captain Anne Donovan of the U.S. Army Nurse Corps heads to the front lines. Along with a small medical unit, she'll provide aid to the soldiers at Hamburger Hill. But when the bloody battle intensifies, and Donovan's chief surgeon is critically wounded by sniper fire, this rookie nurse quickly becomes the leader of an emergency operation.

During the War in Iraq, Lieutenant Commander Lester Donovan of the U.S. Navy SEALs must capture a known terrorist near the border of Syria. It's a dangerous mission. Land mines and hostile combatants blanket the area, yet Donovan is undeterred. But when the mission goes awry, this gung-ho commander must learn to keep his cool if he's going to keep his men alive.

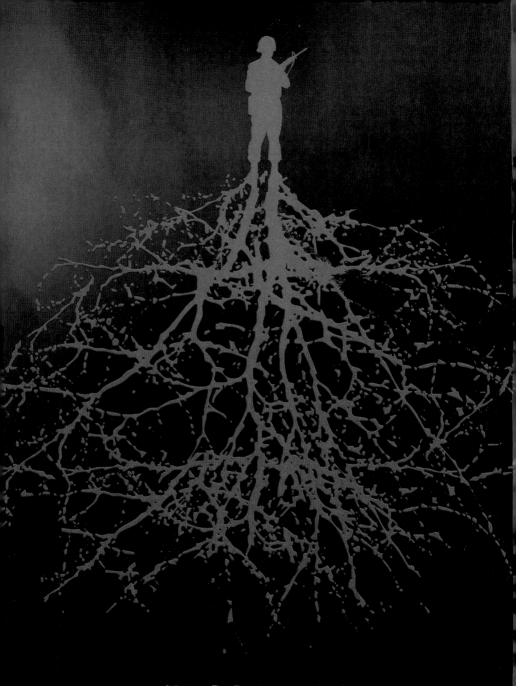

BLOODLINES

www.capstonepub.com